P9-CDI-530

THIS IS HAWKEYE

Written by Clarissa Wong

Illustrated by Andrea Di Vito *and* Rachelle Rosenberg

Based on the Marvel comic book series The Avengers

Los Angeles
New York

marvelkids.com

© 2015 MARVEL

Printed in the United States of America
First Edition, January 2015
1 3 5 7 9 10 8 6 4 2
G658-7729-4-14339
ISBN 978-1-4847-2591-7

SUSTAINABLE
FORESTRY
INITIATIVE

Certified Chain of Custody
Promoting Sustainable Forestry

www.sfiprogram.org
SFI-01415

The SFI label applies to the text stock

This is Clint.

Clint is Hawkeye.

Hawkeye is a Super Hero.

Clint was not always a Super Hero.
He used to work in the circus.

He learned how to use
a bow and arrow there.
He was not very good at first.

Clint practiced every day.
He wanted to be the best.

Clint became a perfect shot.
People called him Hawkeye!

He could shoot very high.

He could shoot while upside down.

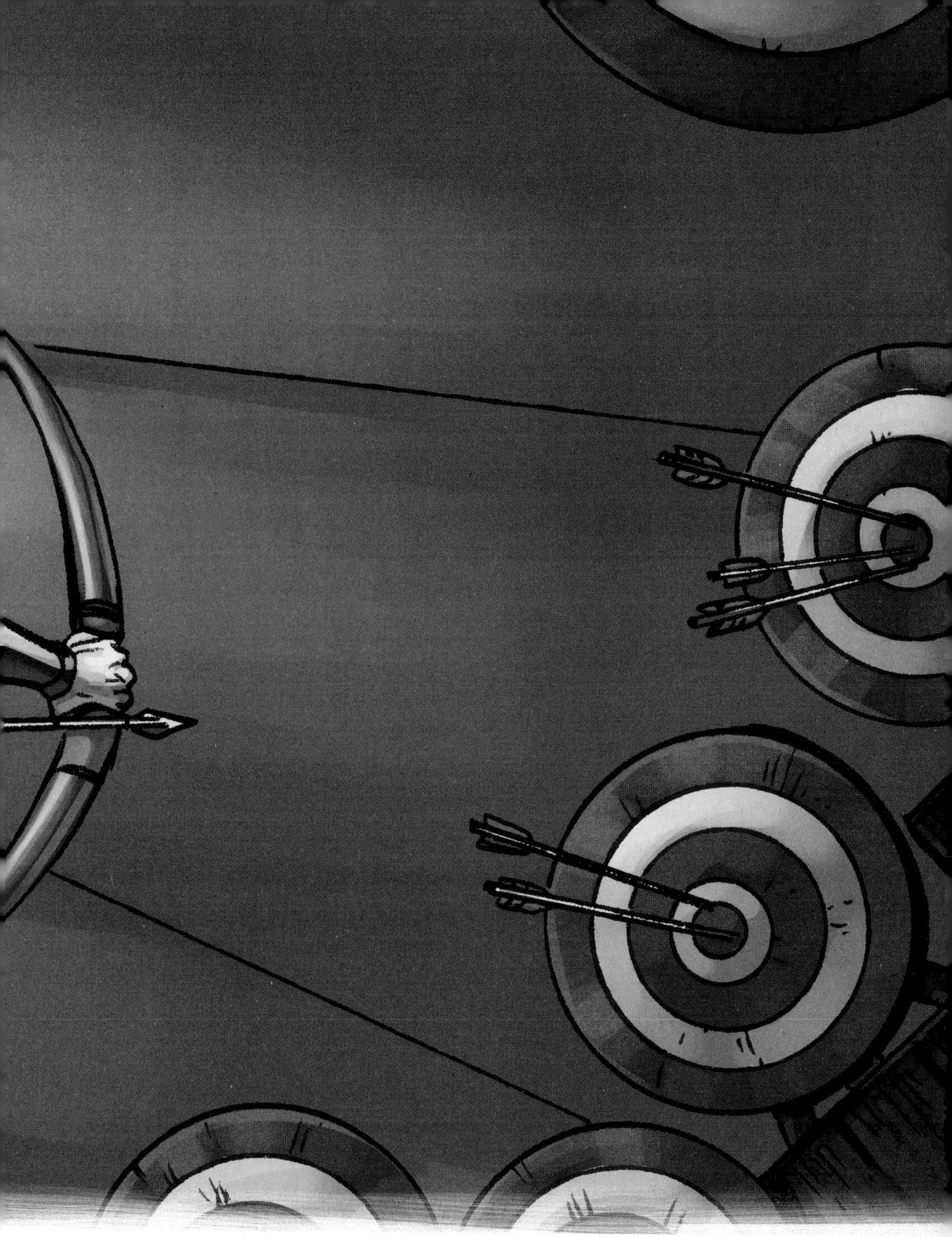

He could make any shot.

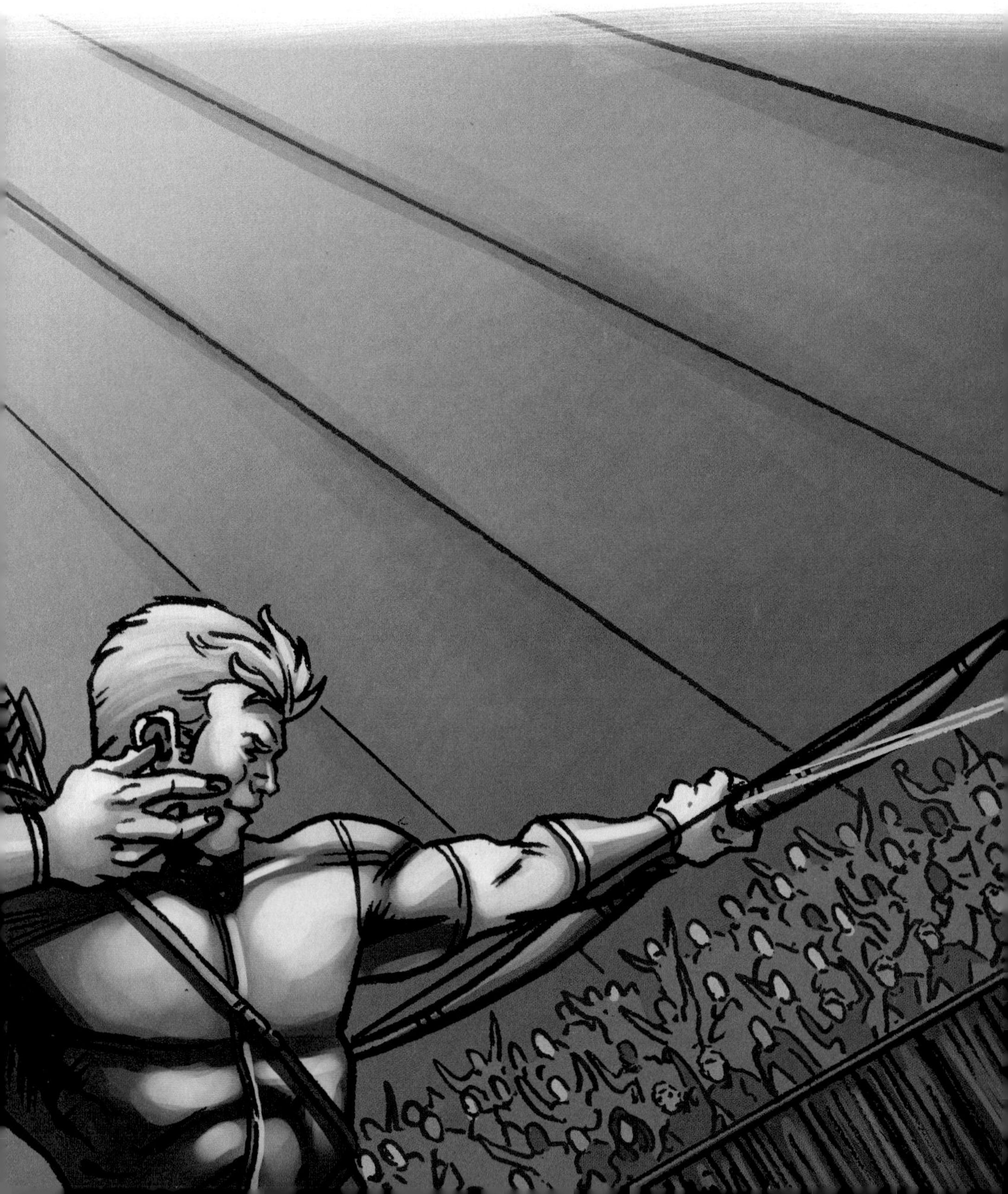

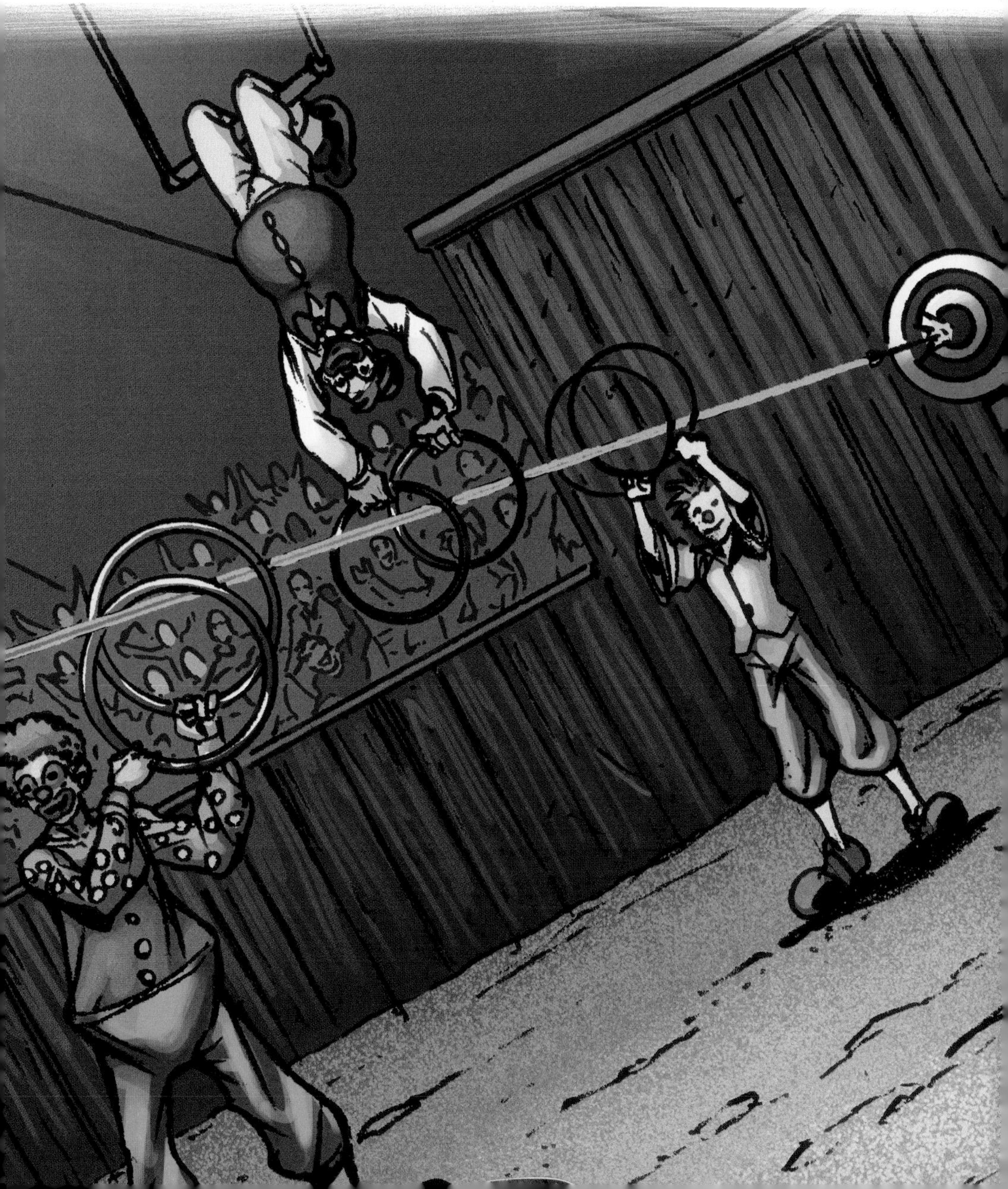

People came from far away
to see him!

He was the most popular act
in the circus.

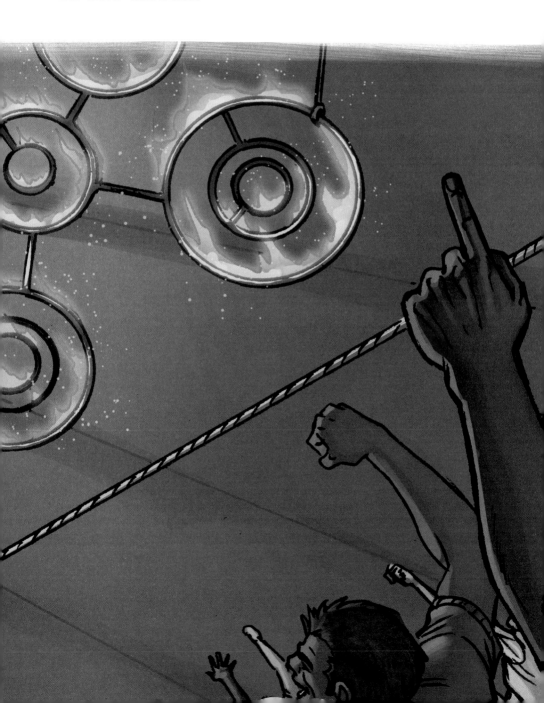

One day, Nick Fury came to see
the famous archer.
Fury was the leader of a group
called S.H.I.E.L.D.

Fury asked Hawkeye to be part of S.H.I.E.L.D.!
Hawkeye is now a spy.
He is a secret agent.

He works with Black Widow.
They make a great team.

Together, they stop villains!

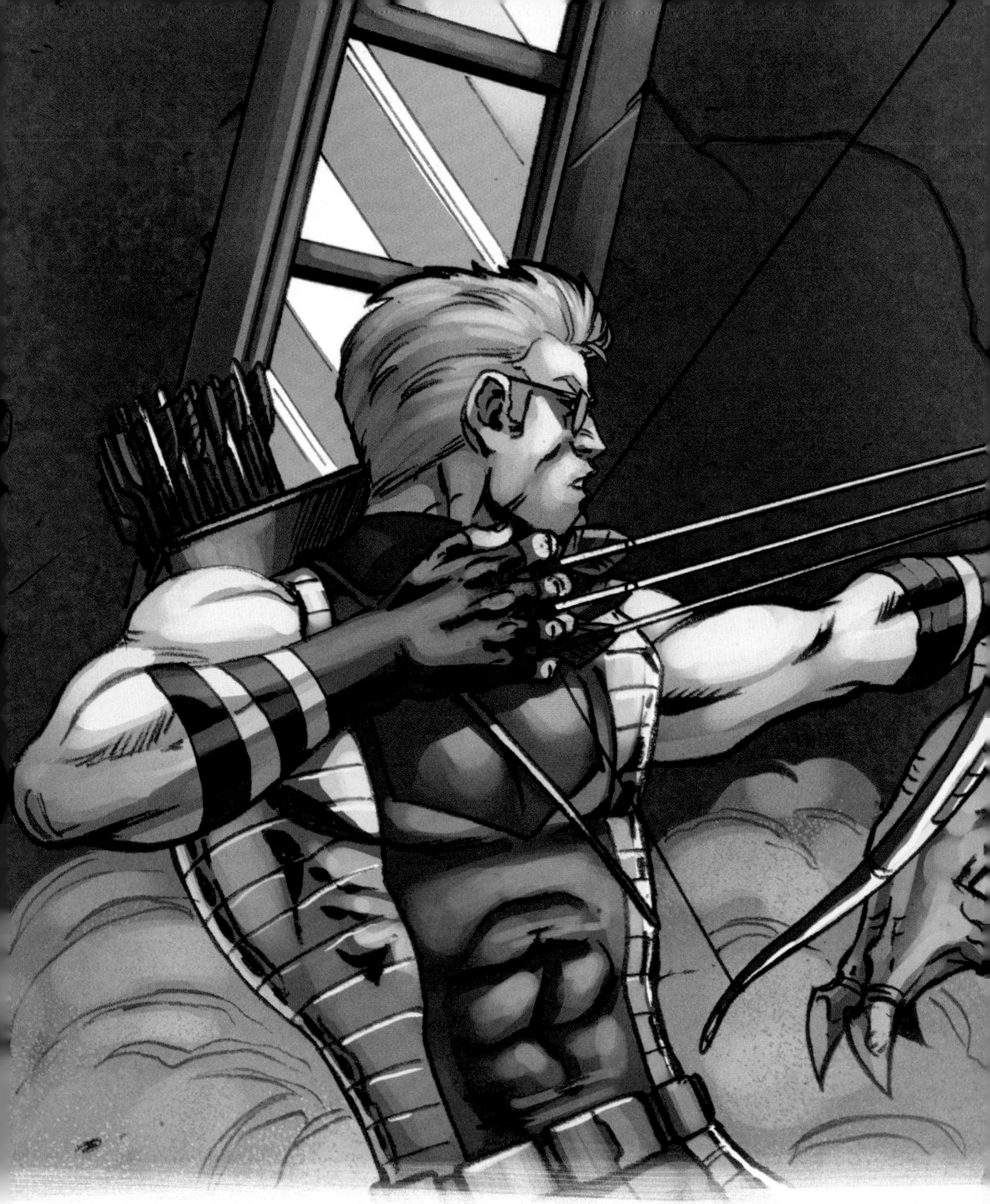

Watch out, villains!

Here come Hawkeye
and Black Widow!

They are best friends.
They joke around together.

They became Avengers, too.

Hawkeye can take out
crooks...

...even if they are far away!

Iron Man helps Hawkeye
get a good angle.
They work as a team.

Hawkeye can get to places
no one else can.

He is always there to help!

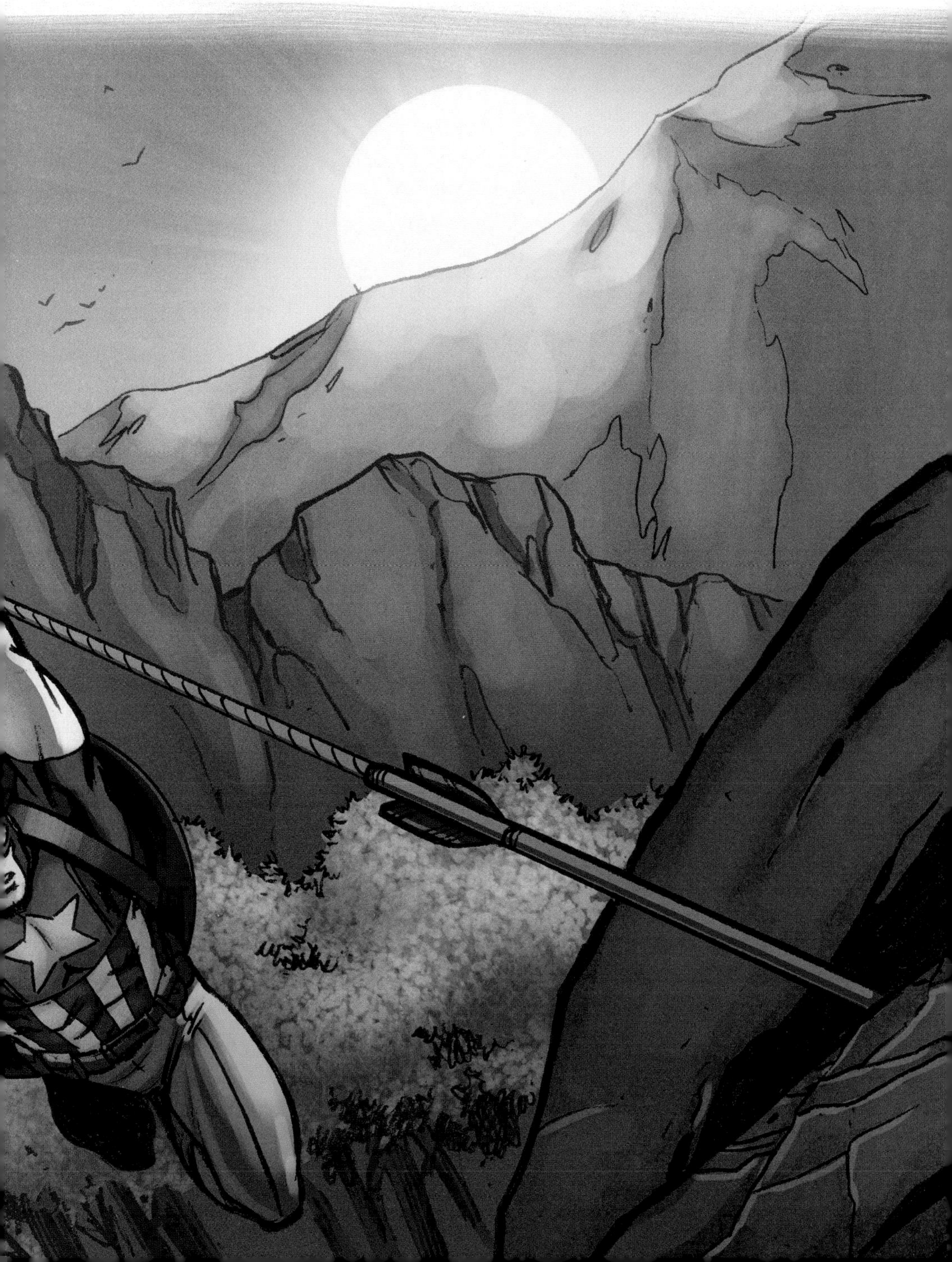

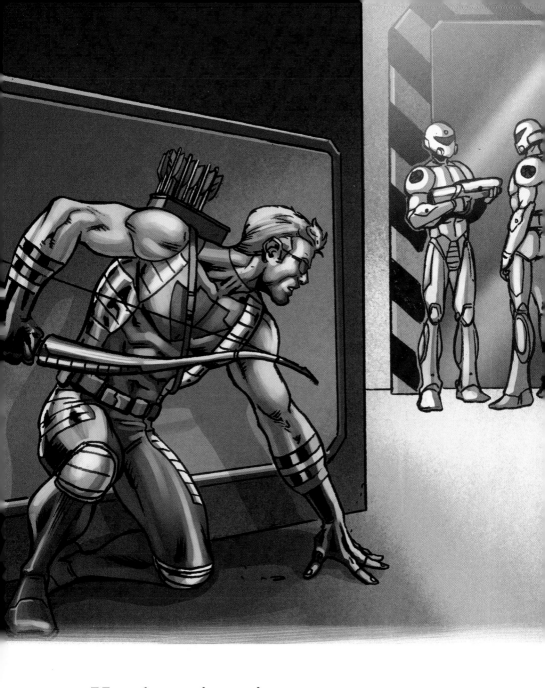

Hawkeye is quiet.
No one hears him coming.

He never misses his target.

That is because he is Hawkeye!